DEC – – 2019

D1093001

WITHDRAWN
ESTES VALLEstes Valley Library
LIBRARY

This book belongs to:

_____

_____

_____

Copyright © 2013 by Lucy Cousins
Lucy Cousins font copyright © 2013 by Lucy Cousins

Illustrated in the style of Lucy Cousins by King Rollo Films, Ltd.

Maisy™. Maisy is a trademark of Walker Books Ltd., London.

All rights reserved. No part of this book may be reproduced, transmitted,
or stored in an information retrieval system in any form or by any means, graphic, electronic, or mechanical,
including photocopying, taping, and recording, without prior written permission from the publisher.

First U.S. paperback edition 2015

Library of Congress Catalog Card Number 2012942386
ISBN 978-0-7636-6480-0 (hardcover)
ISBN 978-0-7636-7749-7 (paperback)

19 APS 10 9 8 7 6

Printed in Humen, Dongguan, China

This book was typeset in Lucy Cousins.
The illustrations were done in gouache.

Candlewick Press
99 Dover Street
Somerville, Massachusetts 02144

visit us at www.candlewick.com

Maisy Learns to Swim

Lucy Cousins

CANDLEWICK PRESS

Maisy is going swimming today. Time to get ready!

Do you have everything you need, Maisy?

Eddie and Tallulah are coming too.

Eddie is already wearing his goggles. "I'm an underwater diver!" he says.

Maisy and Tallulah get ready
in the changing room.
It's so busy!

Nice swimsuit, Tallulah!

The pool looks very big.
Maisy dips her toes in first.
Ooh, it's freeeezing!

Maisy and Tallulah get
into the pool slowly.

The water goes swish-swash, splish-splash. It feels nice!

Their swim teacher is named **Poppy**. She's a really good swimmer.

"Let's warm up," **Poppy** says. "Wiggle your toes and lift your arms in the air!"

Next, everyone holds on to their kickboards and kicks their feet.

Hee, hee!

Yipee!

Wow, it's so noisy!

Now it's time to try floating!

Maisy pushes her belly up to the ceiling and stretches her arms out like a starfish.

Poppy shows everyone how to blow bubbles. Tallulah takes a deep breath . . .

puts her nose in the water...
and blows out as hard as she can—
Blup-blup-blup!

Maisy wants to try too.

1-2-3 ...

blup-blup-blup!

Look at all the bubbles!

"Well done, everyone!" says Poppy.
"That was a great lesson.
Up the ladder we go!"

Maisy feels shivery out of the water, so she wraps herself up in a fluffy towel. Aaaah, that's better!

She needs a nice warm shower.

"Me too," says Maisy.
"Floating is my
favorite!"

Now it's time for a snack!
"When is our next lesson?" says Maisy.
She can't wait to
go swimming
again!